This book belongs to...

~~~~~~~~~~~~~~~~~~~~

S.A.

ISBN: 978-1-0931-4270-9
Design and typesetting by Philip Bell (www.beachybooks.com)

Set in Adobe Caslon Pro, and Grandma

The Hungry Fox

by

Shirley Adams

MiceElf

"OHHH!" sighed Foxy
feeling quite glum.
"There's a big empty hole
right here in my tum."

He stood on a rock,
to be high off the ground
and cast his bright beady
eyes all around.

"I'M HUNGRY!" cried Foxy

"I'm in need of some dinner.

I'm wasting away... getting thinner and thinner.

I want something now!

I want something **hasty!**

I want a nice treat!

I want something **tasty!**"

"I'm ever so hungry.
It's well past my luncheon.

I am **SO** peckish
I need something to
crunch on!"

Then a short sudden
movement from under a log
revealed to his gaze a little
hedgehog.

"**OOOH!**" said Foxy, "I think that you'll do.
I fancy a plateful of hedge-hoggy stew!"

"**NO! STOP!**" cried the hedgehog.

"What if a prickle got stuck in your tum and started to tickle?

"And how would you feel if some of my fleas jumped up your nose and you started to sneeze?"

Foxy thought for a moment, then shook his head.
"A Tickly Tum and a Fleasily Sneeze?
No thanks!"
He said.

Foxy asked hedgehog, "I'd like your advice
What do **YOU** eat when you want something nice?"

"Ah," said the hedgehog,
"If you'd like to see,
stay and have some lunch
with me."

"Ugh! Thanks, but no thanks!" muttered Foxy
As he turned up his nose at a big pile of worms.

"I couldn't eat those – they're full of germs!"

Now rabbits are generally not very brave
a fact that was missed by a bunny called Dave.

And never once thinking that he could be ate
had teamed up with Foxy and became his best mate.

But the hungry fox thought, "I have a hunch. that Dave looks quite tasty!

Oh! It's been ages and ages since I had some lunch."

"**NO! STOP!**" shouted Dave
"It's really not cricket to think of your friend
as just a meal ticket."

Foxy thought for a moment then nodded his head
"It's wrong to eat a friend," he said.

So Foxy asked Dave, "I would like your advice.
What do **YOU** eat when you want something nice?"

"HMMM…" replied Dave. "I think I would settle
for a carrot, some lettuce… and … a juicy young
nettle."

"No thanks!" said Foxy, "I'm not terribly keen
I'd prefer to eat something… a little less green!"

The Fox had a plan that he thought was ideal
as to how he could find a nice dinner to steal.

He ran to the farm at Blueberry Thatch
quite sure he could finally grab a good catch.

Hungrily he sniffed the air... the smell of food was everywhere.

He slid across the stony ground careful not to make a sound...

He took one step and then three more...
and tiptoed past the farmhouse door...

He gathered some feathers to make a disguise,
so clever you'd never believe your own eyes.

Then hid behind a tree to wait.
He'd soon be through the hen house gate.

Then very strangely Foxy attempted to cluck,
but the fox speaking **'Chicken!'**... sounded more like a **Duck!**

The farmer's wife heard this peculiar cry.
She said, "I spy a fox with a glint in his eye!"

"**NO! STOP!**" cried the old lady, "Don't be so fast!
One of MY chickens will be YOUR last!"

And there amid a great commotion…
She fired the gun with one swift motion…

BANG went the gun!

BANG!

BANG!

BANG!

Foxy ran fast — and his poor ears **RANG-RANG-RANG!**

The Fox ran all the way home, his hungry tum aching.
He felt battered and bruised and couldn't stop shaking.

But Dave who had thought it would end in disaster
soothed him with pink lemonade and a plaster.

He said, "As you've had an awful fright,
I thought we'd have a treat tonight...
It's hasty and tasty and ever so easy...

We made a big pizza...

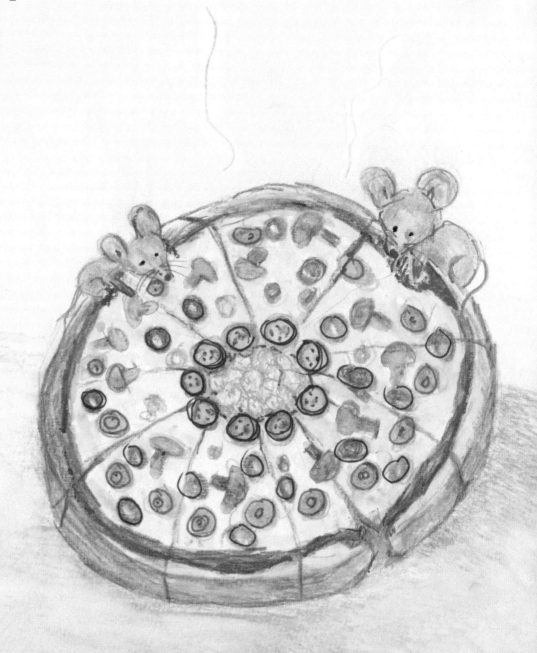

Extra cheesy!

Printed in Poland
by Amazon Fulfillment
Poland Sp. z o.o., Wrocław

49700439R10016